LIFE IN THE ETHNIC INDIA:

A COLLECTION OF SHORT STORIES

MISHTI | ANANYA | INIKA | SRISHTI

Contents

Acknowledgements

We, Inika Mohile, Mishti Agarwal, Srishti Agarwal and Ananya Singh would like to acknowledge the extraordinary debt that we pay to all the people, who in some way or the other played a role in being an aid for us in writing our first book.

First and foremost we would like to extend our gratitude towards the Almighty because of whom the thought of writing a book came into our mind.

Secondly, we would like to thank our parents who have been a source of encouragement and upliftment throughout the process of writing this book.

Thirdly, we would like to thank the authors of the books that we have read, as it were these books that lighted a spark within us to write a book of our own.

We would also like to thank the readers of our book, that you chose our book and we hope you love it!

Last but not the least, we would like to express our gratitude for being a citizen of such an exuberant nation which has so many stories to tell.

~Members of MIRIAN CLUB

CHAPTER ONE

THE HIDDEN WARRIORS

It would not be very late before the dark of the night began to spread in the skies. Dharam, a small boy of 11, had gone to a nearby shop and one wrong turn got him to loose his way and here he was, at the time of dusk, wandering in the forest of Kamyaka and every step seemed to take him even deeper inside. Before leaving, his mother had warned him of two things, not to wander uselessly in the kingdom and not to talk with any of the knights of the Kauravas, they were evil people, unrighteous and wicked. Yet he had wandered into the streets of his kingdom and on losing the track, he had asked his way to one of the guards of the main gate of the palace of Kauravas. They must have told him the wrong way, and now, it had been a whole day walking without food and water and night was about to set. His parents would be worried and so would his 5 brothers and 3 sisters. But he could not walk anymore. He was going to faint. He was too tired to take even a single step ahead. His legs could not bear his weight and he fell to the ground, unconscious.

On regaining his consciousness and his senses, he found six people staring down at him, a woman and five men, one of them being exceptionally large.

"Who is he, Aarya?" asked the woman.

"I don't know, Panchali. I found this boy unconscious deep within the jungle when I was looking for water, Brother Yudhishthir had sent me to get it. I think he is lost." said the large man.

"I believe that is true Bheem, he really is lost." said another man.

" Or," said yet another " he could be a spy sent by Duryodhan to spy on us. You know brother Yudhishthir, we need to be careful, very, very careful as this is the last year of our exile and we soon will have to go into hiding."

"Arjun," said the previous one," we cannot always suspect everyone. And even if he is a spy, he was found unconscious deep within the jungle and we can see he needs food and water. According to our dharm, we must help everyone we can. And he needs our help, we cannot refuse that."

"But Brother Yudhishthir!"

"Arjun! We cannot deny help to this boy."

Then turning to Dharam, the man named Yudhishthir said,"Child, what is your name?"

"My name is Dharam. Who - who are you all?"

"We," continued Yudhishthir, "are the residents, of this forest. Tell us child, where are you from?"

Dharam was about to answer but a growl of hunger from his stomach spoke for itself, making it obvious that his prior need was food.

"Panchali, our guest seems to be hungry. Is there any food left which can still be eaten?"

"Yes Aarya!" replied the woman, "There were some rice left

after dinner, and by God's grace they still must be fresh. Let me get them."

The woman went into the cottage and though it was night, Dharam could still see that among the five pairs of eyes staring down at him, Yudhishthir was smiling and it seemed he would be glad if he could be of some help while the others standing beside Yudhishthir seemed to be questioning with suspicion.

After eating the rice hungrily and drinking enough water to quench the thirst of the whole day, Dharam continued with his introduction, "I am Dharam, I live in Indraprastha, I had gone out of my house to roam the streets and got lost in the kingdom. On arriving at the palace's main gates, I asked one of the guards the way and he showed me this way, I kept on walking to this way through the day hoping to arrive at my house soon but I never did, my mother had warned me that the Kauravas and those who are with Kauravas are evil, and these wicked people showed me the wrong way, and now, I am lost in this dark forest. I don't know if I will ever be able to see my family again." Saying this, Dharam began to cry.

The woman stepped forward to comfort the child by softly rubbing his back.

"So," said Yudhishthir "it is clear that the boy is from Indraprastha and wishes to go back, we have to help him. Now listen, you all will stay here on guard, and I, with this boy will go to Indraprastha, drop this boy at his home, and come back."

"No Brother!" said the large man, "I certainly don't agree. Why should you take the trouble when I am here at your service. I will do it, I will go!"

"No Brother!" now said the man who had first showed his suspicion, "Why should any of you go when I am here, ready to do anything. I will go with this boy and return before the dawn."

"No, my dear Brothers, I don't agree with this." said the one who seemed to be younger than the preceding one, "It should be my job to do this."

"No!" interrupted the youngest one, "I'll go, I'll do this!"

"In the name of the Gods, why are we taking so much time to decide this, it will not be long before Surya Devta shows himself up in the sky. Now no need to decide, I am going myself." said the woman.

"No Panchali!" cried all men together.

After a short silence, Arjun said, "Let me go Brother."

"Ok Arjun." Said Yudhishthir finally, "But remember, you must return before the dawn and no one shall see you."

"As you say, Brother." said Arjun and left with the boy.

Now walking in the deep forest in the dark did not seem as scary as it would have been had it not been for Arjun and his talks that kept Dharam distracted.

"Please tell me who you are exactly! Or else, how will I tell to anyone who helped me in the forest." Said Dharam.

"You don't need to tell anyone." chuckled Arjun

"Oh, please! Okay, I promise, I won't tell anyone except my mother."

"And who will your mother tell?"

"No one, literally, no one."

"Okay, then tell your mother that there were five men and a woman in the forest who lived in a cottage who helped you."

This way, Dharam did not realise how quickly he found himself at the doorstep of his house.

"But, I don't even know the way! How did I reach? And it is not even dawn yet." Dharam exclaimed in surprise and turned to his side. No one was there. He turned to the other side, and to the back, no one was there. The man called

Arjun had left. His wonder soon faded away as he heard the sorrowful cries coming from his home. He rushed inside and to everyone's surprise and gratefulness, he was alright! "Where had you been?" asked his mother, hugging him tightly. "I'll tell you mother." said he as he took her to a corner.

After hearing the account of what had happened with Dharam, the mother said.

"The people you met in the forest were the great warriors, the Pandavas."

CHAPTER TWO

THE BUSINESSMAN

The sorching heat of the sun has set down, leaving the people in relief. The shops at the fair were now brighten up with lights. The music soothed the souls of the visitors of the fair. The hustling of the people and the shopkeepers promoting their products participated in the ambience of the handicrafts exhibition. The people wandered the aisles of the temporary shops with no regrets of coming here. The products were delicate with fine quality and a variety of designs.

Sitting at a shop, a 30 year old woman selling paintings was upset; as she made no profit since the last two days. The paintings were indeed beautiful but very expensive, which the people of that town didn't prefer to buy. She regretted putting her stall in this fair. That evening, a young man, about 26 years old, who seemed like a tourist, approached her. He was tall and had long hair tied in a pony. He looked at the paintings in awe. "Magnificent!" He smiled and looked at her, "how much is it?", he asked pointing at a painting. The woman replied,"900 Rupees sir. She assumed that he is interested in the product, and began giving more details," It's made of good quality canvas and painted with high quality paints, hence it cannot cost less than 900 rupees sir." The man replied with a short laugh," Oh no, don't worry about that, I don't shop by looking at the prices. " "Well, I have more paintings, if you would like to see. She took out 3 paintings from the back. "These are the 3 best paintings sold last year.Mandala was the best selling among the three."

"Are you reselling these, or you painted them?"

"Of course sir, I painted them."

"Oh, so how much have you earned yet in this fair?"

"Well sir, you won't believe, you are my first costumer since the last 2 days.", she said miserably.

"Oh I'm so sorry. But then, why don't you sell them at a low cost? You know, people here won't buy such items at this cost here."

"Well, I have a business strategy." She told him, though having none. Then realizing, why he is asking such questions, she asked, changing the topic, "Shall I pack this painting for you sir?"

"Oh, I am thinking to buy all the three of them, if you sell them to me at 300Rs each."

"No sir, that's not even half the price of one."

"Okay, make it 400 for each."

"Sir, I haven't had a profit since last two days. Please understand."

He ignored her."So, from where do you get all the supplies for making your products? I mean, the quality is really good."

She didn't want to tell, but her tongue slipped, "Painting_works on Instagram" Shopkeeper smiled lightly, that it was hardly visible. "Oh sorry, I didn't hear that.",he pretended he didn't listen.

The lady changed the topic again,"Sir, which painting should I pack?"

"Oh sorry, I am not interested anymore. I would've bought all of them for 900."

With that, he left the lady, who later agreed to take 900 for all 3, but the man ignored her again.The man joined his companion, who was waiting there having no clue what his friend was up to. He asked him, "What were you doing there for 30 minutes, when you didn't buy anything?

"Let's go, I just got some great ideas for my business." He grinned and left.

CHAPTER THREE

LONG JOURNEY SHORT

Ankita wiped the sweat off her forehead as she sat on the train from Delhi to Jaipur. She was finally going home, after a long time of two months, she was going back home for a fortnight. How happy would her mother be to see her unexpectedly waiting at her door. Among the others who boarded the train carriage, a small family of four struggled to find seat. Soon they found one and were sitting all smushed into each other when the lady spotted the empty seat beside Ankita and asked her elder daughter, around nine years old or so, to go sit there. It was odd as the woman had not asked if Ankita was okay with it or not. Ankita, however, knew how soon she would get bored and did not mind the company she had been gifted. The train had only advanced 20 minutes when the girl spoke up "Hi!!". Ankita was surprised at the unusually kind voice of the girl. She replied "Hi! What's your name?"

"Yashvi."

"Nice name! What does it mean?"

"Umm! I don't know. Maybe queen or princess or something. Oh yeah! It must be 'Beautiful Queen'. "

Ankita tried hard not to laugh. She had stayed in Delhi for 9 weeks and hadn't seen such a blabbermouth. She was sure that she was not going to get bored this journey now that she had someone to talk to.

"What is your name?" Yashvi said.

"I'm Ankita."

"Hmm, it must be something related to a kite."

"A kite?" Asked Ankita shockingly.

"Yes! Because it has got the word kit (kite) in it."

"Uhh, Okay!

"Where are you from anyways?"

"Well, I'm from Kamandra."

"Kamndra? Where's that?"

"Oh, you don't know! Never mind."

"Well you gotta tell me where is it. Or else, how will I know?"

"Okay!" said the little girl, " It is a beautiful kingdom with a beautiful palace where I live. It is my kingdom and I'm the princess, you know."

"Nice."

Said Ankita, now taking interest in Yashvi's talks.

"And you know," the little girl continued, "back in my palace, we have discovered a diamond the size of a mountain."

"Ohh!"

"Yes!!""And you know, I've got power! I can read minds."

"Ohh, well then tell what am I thinking."

"Umm, you are thinking, that I am very beautiful. Right?"

"Ohh, Wow! How did you know?"

"Because I can read minds!"

The two laughed until they had a fit.

Yashvi asked,"Where are you from anyways?"

Ankita replied,"I am from Jaipur."

"So tell me something about Jaipur!" exclaimed the curious child.

"Jaipur is also known as the pink city, did you know? " Started Ankita

" Wow! "

" It is also known as the Royal City of Rajasthan. It has got many forts, palaces and magnificent architecture. We wear colourful outfits and marvellous jwellery on any occasion. People dance with lit diyas on their heads, that's Ghoomar by the way. We have fairs and festivals. Jaipur, where I live, is the perfect example for if you want to see the western tradition and culture."

Who would have thought that a 6 hour boring trip in a typical Indian train from Delhi to Jaipur would become so exciting with a little company by a little kid. That's the beauty of things so common that the eyes which refuse to see miss all the fun. That's the beauty of India in its depth.

CHAPTER FOUR

AN INEXPLICABLE TALE

It was the middle of June, 2015. Garima was at her Grandma's. One thing you could always count on, Garima had never spent a June away from her grandmother (maternal). Every year, twenty days in the sixth month would be reserved for a visit to her grandmother! So, it was the middle of June, 2015. She was at her Grandma's. It was a refreshing evening, cool breeze was swishing across her face, and she, her 8 year old self, was sitting under the only banyan tree there was, and still is, in the village. She was reading one of her comics there, and was so lost in it that she didn't notice an old man who had walked up to her, and was looking at the book she was reading. He was really very old, wearing a white casual Indian dhoti, and it was surprising to her that he didn't wear spectacles. Garima looked up at him and saw that he was taking utmost pleasure in examining the cover of the book. She stood up and offered him to sit there, if he wished to. He slowly leaned forward, put the walking stick he was using on the ground, carefully, and sat in such a way that the trunk of the tree supported his back. He then asked her to sit too, which, she did. He then asked that what exactly was she reading. Garima told him it was a comic book written in English. As she had seen, some of her friends in the village found it difficult to understand the language, she had clearly underestimated the wisdom of the old man. He said that he wanted to take a look at the book so she gave it to him. He flipped through the pages rapidly and swiftly, twice and handed it back to her, saying that it was an interesting book. He then looked away at the hand pump that was there to his left. Garima was sitting at his right, wondering whether he had actually understood anything in the book, or he was just trying to make her think that he understood. He then turned to her and again asked for the book and said, "I have not read anything in English for a really long time now. Let me see if I still have a good hold on the language or not." And he said it in such a fluent manner that one could have easily mistaken him for a native of the Great Britain. Garima was flabbergasted at this. Just at the moment when she was thinking whether the old man could speak English or not, he had proved it to her.. could he read minds? Garima handed him the book again. He opened the first page that was the 'Acknowledgements' and started to read. Within seconds as she heard him read, she developed great respect for him, as if, she somehow knew him. He finished reading and handed her back the book, and said, "I think I can still read, can't I." Garima smiled, unsure of what to say. He asked for a glass of water. The little girl ran inside the house, leaving her book behind. She saw that her Mother and Grandma were discussing something important. Garima told them that there was an old man who wanted a glass of water. Her grandmother looked reluctant at the idea of serving complete strangers and said that she could help him draw water from the hand pump. Garima was still thinking of what to say exactly so that the old man doesn't feel bad when to her surprise, she reached outside and found him waiting for her at the hand pump. Did he just read her mind, again? She could only smile. She reached out to the handle and swung it up to down as he drank water. He then came up to her, bent low, and touched her feet. Garima stepped back hastily and asked him that why did he do that when he was much older than her! He said that he had read her book so she deserved the respect. Then unable to think of anything to say, some words really senseless to the situation shot out, "May I know your name?" He chuckled and said, "People call me Mangal Singh." He then went back to the tree, with slow and steady steps, reached out for his bamboo stick which he used to walk with, and left, left her shocked. Garima was sure that she had heard the name before. She rushed inside and asked her Mom, who was now watering the plants in the garden. "Mom, random question, do you know who is Mangal Singh?". Her mother was kind of doubtful, then she said, "Well, he was your grandfather." Garima was thunderstruck. Her grandfather had passed away just a few days before she was born!

CHAPTER FIVE

A SUMMER HOLIDAY

Summer holidays arrived and no one could be happier than Rohan. He almost jumped off his seat when the last period's bell rung and the teacher said,"Okay kids, Happy Holidays!!" This was his first holidays, and what he has heard from his elder cousins is that holidays were the most exciting part of the year. We travel,don't study and roam here and there.

He couldn't wait to reach his home and ask his parents about the plans they have made for him.

Soon he was in the kitchen with his gleamed eyes staring at his mother and chubby cheeks shining with a wide smile of excitement, waiting for his mother to turn to him.

"What happened child?", said Rohan's mother, still busy in her work.

"Mom, where are we going these holidays?"

Finally she turned to him.

"Nowhere"

"What!! Why! Summer holidays are started. Aren't we supposed to travel?"

"No! Your father isn't free this summer. So we would not go anywhere."

"Mumma, will I not have fun?"

"Beta, yes you will, I will teach you art, so that you can do better art."

"Well, can't I join art classes?", his eyes almost like a puppy pleading.

"Oh, you wanna go out in the scorching heat and practice art? And why don't you wanna learn from me?"

He didn't reply and went to his room. He was sad; and the thoughts of him studying and his friends enjoying haunted him.

It was evening, and he was completing his math homework, when suddenly the bell rung, and he ran towards the gate as he knew it was his father.

"Papa!!",his wide smile on his small lips and chubby cheeks made his father squeeze his cheeks tightly.

"Hello Rohan beta."

"Papa, tell mumma to atleast let me go out and have fun with my friends, if we aren't travelling."

"Really? You didn't go out today?"

"Nooooooo....." he almost cried.

"Let me ask your mom."

He asked his mother the reason for this treatment with the little child on his first summer vacations ever.

She wispered in his ear, " I am not telling him that we are going to Jaipur, so that he completes his homework beforehand doesn't leaves it for me in the end."

"Okay, but atleast let him go out and play."

"Yes,yes", she said, continuing her work, as she realized her mistake.

Then Rohan's father went to him and asked him to bring the bag lying on the table of living room and open it.

"ICE CREAM....!", he shouted at the top of his voice. "Yayyyyy, papa you are the best."

"Okay come on, let's have it after dinner."

Rohan wispered in his ear, so that his mother does not listen,"Please just one. " He wispered back,"Okay."

After dinner he was having his second ice-cream, writing on a paper from his other hand, all the fun things he would do this summer, unknown of the fact, that the paper will be of no use after he comes to know the great surprise he'll get for his hardwork of 1 week completing his homework.

Few days later, Rohan wokeup by the hustling at the house. He streched and got out of his bed. As he came out of the room, he noticed some suticases beside the table. He was confused, and thought that his mother might be cleaning the store room. Soon after, his mother came out of the store room. She didn't expect his presence, and realizing now, that the surprise has been disclosed, she smiled at her and said,"Child, I am sure, you might have done your homework. We planned this surprise for you that we are going to jaipur, as.." "Jaipur!!", he didn't let her complete her sentence. "Really? oh mommy, all these days of hardwork had brought me so much happiness today.",he hugged her tightly. Mother smiled back and and kissed her on his forehead. "Okay, now go brush your teeth and have a bath.We are leaving tomorrow so help me pack the stuff." Rohan nodded and rushed to the bathroom. Mother took one of the suitcases and went to Rohan's room;opened the cupboard and packed his bag. Soon Rohan came and helped her mother.

The day was over, and they were now in the train. Rohan took the window seat. Mother noticed his happiness and told his father,"The surprise didn't fail. Look at Rohan. He seems so happy." Father smiled back,"Yes." In 6 hours they were at Jaipur. They then checked in at the hotel and rested for a while after the long tiring journey.

The upcoming days were memorable for Rohan. On the first day of their trip they went to the HEART OF THE OLD CITY, CITY PALACE. His father told Rohan, "Rohan, protected by huge guard walls, this fairy-tale-like structure is still the home of Jaipur's modern-day royal family, and is more extravagant and enchanting than you might imagine." Rohan widened his eyes when he listened to his father. Next they went to JANTAR MANTAR. "Mumma, it's just a bunch of larger-than-life sculptures.Looks like an art gallery." "Beta,this is not an art gallery.It's a special collection of astronomical tools started by Rajput ruler Jai Singh II to measure the heavens nearly 300 years ago." "Oh wow!" Then they came across a massive sun dial, and his father explained,"The observatory's massive sun dial, known as Samrat Yantra, is particularly striking. At 27 meters tall, it casts a huge shadow that accurately measures time down to two seconds." Rohan didn't understand a thing, except that the sun dial is known as Samrat Yantra. Then they hired a guide to understand how the structures work. In the evening they enjoyed the famous PYAAZ KACHORI."Onion in the kachori; very creative!!", Rohan said relishing the kachori.

Next day, Rohan enjoyed the Palace of Breeze, Hawa Mahal. They hired another guideand he told them that it was built to resemble the crown of Hindu god Krishna, to the geometric accents and rows of tiny windows. "The landmark was built in 1799 to allow royal ladies to watch festivals on the street without being seen by the public.", the guide continued. After the tour, his father asked the guide,"Can you tell us about the markets?Is it worth watching.?" "Sir,Jaipur is a mecca for souvenirs. Markets in the Pink City brim with everything from costume jewelry to embroidered textiles, cobalt blue pottery, and Rajasthani puppets.Johari Bazar is a jewelry-lover's paradise. The market glitters from top to bottom with dozens of shops selling everything from costume jewelry to fine gold and silver. No matter what your budget is, you'll find something beautiful to take home from here." The family was amazed by the fact and they decided to take home with them many things along with a puppet which Rohan insisted.

After a whole one week of travel, the family came back home. They were all very tired. At night, Rohan was lying on his bed feeling really satisfied. He was thinking all sorts of way he would describe his holidays to his friends and about the list of fun activities which was of no use in the holidays.

CHAPTER SIX

MAGICAL FINGERS THEY DIDN'T KNOW ABOUT

It was a delightful afternoon when Suchita's family decided to go out for lunch in one of the most orthodox and traditional, yet a widely famous restaurant in "The Sleepless City of India" ,Madurai. Madurai is not called so because of any issues that the city faces, but because of the lively lifestyle of the people who love to work and tend to keep the charisma of celebration all the time.

Suchita's mother ran a homestay and this time they had tourists who came from Canada. These tourists were always very inquisitive about Indian culture and thus it was decided that they would be taken to a completely authentic South Indian restaurant. After a twenty minute long journey filled with lots of chit chat, they reached the restaurant. Suchita's father placed the order and they were eagerly waiting for the food to arrive.

"Here's your order sir" said the waiter when he brought the sustenance, "We hope you enjoy your meal." The food came served in a freshly plucked Banana leaf and it was evident by the tourist's expression, that they weren't able to figure out how to eat the meal. It was then when they saw that Suchita's family had started to devour the food happily using their hands. No spoon, no fork, no cutlery at all. Just hands! And the tourists were completely taken aback by this quintessential Indian custom.
Suchita noticed their bizzare reaction and said, "Mummy, daddy I think they're assuming that we have our food in a very unhygienic manner. Why don't you tell them?" "Right child, I must tell them" said Suchita's father chuckling on the tourists' reaction.

"So there's a saying in India – Eating food with your hands not only feeds the body but also the mind and the spirit" said Suchita's father. The tourists smiled at this but still felt hesitant to use their hands to eat and said "We don't know where our hands have been". To this Suchita's mother said "Oh dear, don't you remember before bringing you to the table we took you to the hand washing station. We knew you'll be skeptical about having your meal with your hands and that is why we did so. It is completely safe now. You can enjoy your meal stress-free!" The tourists smiled brightly at this and felt relieved. Suchita's mother continued, "The practice of eating with the hands originated within Ayurvedic teachings. The Vedic people believed that our bodies are in sync with the elements of nature and our hands hold a certain power. Ayurvedic texts teach that each finger is an extension of one of the five elements" "Oh honey, let me tell that" interrupted Suchita's hilariously.

“So...Through the thumb comes space, through the forefinger comes air,through the mid-finger comes fire, through the ring finger comes water and Through the pinky finger comes earth. Isn’t that amazing. How just one chunk of food eaten with your fingers provides you with nutrition in abundance!”

The tourists were completely blown away by the information they gained and happily enjoyed the meal just how “it was meant to be”.

All the way back home they kept talking about many more such wonderful traditions in India which aren’t just cultural but also have a deep philosophical and scientific meaning behind them.

CHAPTER SEVEN

THE INDIAN WEDDING

It was a typical Sunday morning in Bangalore,but not for the Sharma's.They were a wealthy family with the most beautiful daughter. Her name was Mitali. It was her wedding day and Mr. Sharma wanted everything to be perfect. "Yes, yes a little bit to the left. Yes perfect" he said. Mrs. Sharma was setting her hair with a mirror in her hand and phone on the other. She was a smug. She went to her room, took some selfies, posted on Instagram and added as the caption: "#exhausted"; though she was the only one who was just doing nothing except of taking selfies. Mitali was just like her mother: self obsessed but she was helping the family. She was having her facial massage and her assistant was telling her schedule of the day which Mitali didn't care about at all. She asked her assistant for a cup of coffee to distract her as she didn't know how to make coffee and it would take her an hour to figure out. After her massage she went to her room to take some beauty sleep.It had been 15 minutes when she woke up, and as she expected the coffee was still not there. Mr. Sharma realised that the caterers still didn't arrive. He called to his servant who was the incharge of calling them. "Where are the caterers? Did you forget to call them? You better have not. I'll fire you." He said angrily. "No sir, that's not the case. I did call them. They said they were busy, but they will manage and come." The servant said which calmed Mr. Sharma.The party was about to start and the caterers still did not arrive. Mr Sharma was worried and furious and he kept taking turns. The servants were calling different places to arrange the caterers. But all of them would deny for such short notice. The guest started to arrive. This made Mrs. Sharma nervous because the last thing she wanted was the reputation to go low. She kept her phone aside and barged in and told her idea. "So the idea is the servants will bring the vessels we need to make the food. Then we'll finalize the menu. And we'll make the food together. One of our servant will bring the spices and food we need. It will be so fun uniting and doing the work together making this occasion special. First Mr. sharma didn't like the idea but seeing that there was no other option left he agreed. He decided to open his Panipuri Stall because it was easy and the only thing he knew. Mrs. Sharma didn't know anything so she decided to open her ice cream stall. The party started, and the priest also arrived. Everyone was enjoying flavory, appetizing and peppery food. Mitali arrived in her wedding dress. And everyone's jaw-dropped. The bride and the groom were sitting on the altar. The priest ask them to stand for the seven circumbulations. When suddenly a question popped out in Mitali's mind. She asked "Sorry to interrupt Pandit ji, but can you please tell the motive of doing them. The priest was flabbergasted. He asked them to sit down. He started " That's a great question dear Mitali, let me start." With this he cleared his throat. "The seven circumbulations or the Satapadi is the true essence of a

Vedic wedding. Only when the bride and the groom take 7 vows keeping the holy pyre as the witness, they are called as married. The bride and the groom hold their hands and take seven rounds around the Agni." Then he asked " Now is it clear child?" "Yes, Pandit Ji, now let's continue." The wedding was over and everyone appreciated them for there unique idea. Everyone was happy on the wedding day.

CHAPTER EIGHT

SAFETY WITH NO LOCKS

"Oh, this is so heart trembling!" exclaimed Jigyasa while reading the newspaper. "Grandma, have you heard of this news?"

"Which news Jiggi?" (Jigyasa's grandma affectionately called her Jiggi).

"Okay, let me tell you. 'Youth, eldest among siblings, killed for resisting theft of his cattle' "

"Oh, that's actually such a terrifying news. One gets killed for protecting what is his" said Jigyasa's grandma. "Times have changed..." continued Jigyasa's grandma "but every cloud has a silver lining. Isn't it? In this world full of thefts, murders, terrorism and so much more there is still one village in India which features establishments with no doors and locks at all." "What! No, that's not possible grandma" said Jigyasa. "I knew you won't believe. But this is true my child. Now pay attention here. There is a village situated in the state of Maharashtra called Shani Shingnapur,which is known for it's popular temple of Shani."

"Oh, I know who Shani is" interrupted Jigyasa. "He's the

Hindu God associated with the planet Saturn. Right Grandma?"

"Right. I'm glad you remember it. So let me continue. As I told you, this village has no locks and no doors at all, just the door frames and despite this, officially no theft was reported in the village. Although there were reports of theft in 2010 and 2011 but even after that, no thefts have been reported for almost more than a decade now!"

" Wow. I can't imagine there could be such a place!" exclaimed Jigyasa.

"Hahaha. Now listen. The temple that I told you about is believed to be a "*jagrut devasthan*" which means that a deity still resides in the temple icon. Villagers believe that god Shani punishes anyone attempting theft.

"Grandma, can you tell something more about the deity?"

"Yes, sure. So The deity here is "Swayambhu" that is self emerged from earth in form of black, imposing stone."

"Ohh" said Jigyasa with wide open eyes.

"Though no one knows the exact period, it is believed that the Swayambhu Shanaishwara statue was found by shepherds of the then local hamlet. It is believed to be in existence at least since the start of Kali Yuga." explained Jigyasa's grandma. "Well, the swayambhu has some historical importance too, but that is a long story and I see that you haven't taken a shower yet! Now go quickly. Take a bath and then we'll continue. But before that my dear Jiggi, I needed a help of yours. Can you please tell me how to share a YouTube link through WhatsApp? I need to send a recipe to Sarla Auntie."

"Oh Grandma. That's so easy. Give me your phone I'll do it" said Jigyasa. "Thank you my child" said Jigyasa's grandma when she kissed Jigyasa on her forehead.

"Well Grandma...." said Jigyasa " I wonder how they keep

the rain away when there are no doors at all!"
Both of them laughed at this and Jigyasa kept on thinking about what could be the history of the Swayambhu.

CHAPTER NINE

BECAUSE ART IN ITSELF IS A STORY

Anamika was occupied in scrolling the internet. After every minute she said "Yes! This is a good one!" and right after this she said, "But no...this is way to ordinary."
She was told to prepare something unique for the occasion of Environment Day in her school. It could be anything like dance, a song, a painting, a speech, a drama. Literally anything! And this is why she was puzzled and the internet was definitely not helping her.

Her elder sister, although engaged in doing something with a lot of paints, called Anamika and said, "What happened? I see you're tossing and turning like a cat on hot bricks." "Uhh" said Anamika with a sheepish grin. "We're told to put together something for Environment Day at school and I'm completely befuddled about what to do. Anyway, forget about it. What's this painting you're making. Looks so different and much more vibrant than what you usually do."

"Well, I tried a lot of art forms from far flung corners of the world. And then few days back, suddenly a thought struck in my mind that why don't I try something from

India. Then I came across this aesthetic form of art. It's Madhubani painting."

"Heavens! This is so stunning and the way you're doing it is just awesome. But...I know you very well. Whenever you make some new art form you try to gather as much as information about it as possible." "So my dear sister, rain a little of your knowledge on your little sister too." said Anamika laughingly.

Anamika's sister chucked and said, "Oh yes my baby sister." "So the Madhubani Painting is a 2500 year old folk art which is said to date back to the time of Ramayana. When King Janaka asked an artist to capture his daughter,Sita's wedding to Prince Rama. These paintings were usually created by women on walls and floors of homes during festivals, ceremonies or special occasions."

"Oh! I never wondered that this had it's origin in such ancient times!" exclaimed Anamika.

"Yes!" said Anamika's sister.

"And you know what Anamika, while I was making this painting, I remembered that three months back when we went to Bihar during our summer break, I saw similar paintings drawn on trees. Oh, and that reminds me to tell you that these paintings owe their origination to Bihar."

"Ahh yes. I remember. We saw the similar paintings when were on the way to Rajnagar. But why were these paintings on the trees. Do you know?"

"Yes I do!" said Anamika's sister excitedly. "Women in those areas use their creativity and tradition to prevent deforestation in the area by making beautiful paintings on trees."

"But how?" asked Anamika with a confused look on her face.

"Let me tell you.These artists adorn the trees with forms of gods and other religious and spiritual symbols like Radha-Krishna, Rama-Sita, scenes from Ramayana and Mahabarata and other mythologies. This instills reverence and preventes the trees from being cut. And till date not a single tree has been cut there. Isn't that amazing!" said Anamika's sister.

"Yes it is!" said Anamika. "Wait a minute. YOU JUST GAVE ME THE BEST IDEA EVER FOR MY SCHOOL WORK. THANK YOU!!" exclaimed Anamika in the loudest and the happiest voice possible.

"How come?" asked her sister.

"I can apprise about Madhubani Painting in my school, tell about the campaign that was commenced by women in the state of Bihar for preventing deforestation, learn how to do Madhubani Painting from you, prepare a few art pieces myself, show them in school and put forward the suggestion of doing Madhubani painting on the trees that are near to our school. What say?" said Anamika joyfully.

"That's a great idea. Go ahead with it." said Anamika's sister.

Anamika thanked her sister and gave her a tight hug. By that time, their mother called them down for lunch and told them that India won the 2020 UNESCO Asia-Pacific Awards for cultural heritage conservation.

Anamika smiled at this and said to herself in a low hushed voice "There's no country as marvelous as mine. I love my India!"

CHAPTER TEN

ONE BUSY AFTERNOON!

It was a hot summer day in Madurai and the scorching heat of the sun was melting the people. Therefore they couldn't stop themselves from having an ice cream to freeze their bodies back. The tampri street was as usual busy in the afternoon as it ever will be the entire year. The fruits and vegetable sellers standing under an umbrella shade, flying away the flies from their fruits and veggies and selling them not losing a penny. The scooters and bikes honking to remove the people out of their way, who were buying grocery from the stores and going to other shops one by one causing crowd. The school nearby was just over and the crowd was even much bigger now. Ice cream shops were now overcrowded with children of school yelling their ice-cream flavours to the shopkeeper. "I want Mango flavour uncle" "Orange uncle", and the frustrated ice-cream seller replied, "I am not Orange okay? Talk properly!" The gang of backbenchers just came out, with one of them clicking group pictures who brought phone with him. "Rahul, go grab and icecream and stand in the middle of the group and make a V with your hand." "V?" "The peace sign man!!"

Soon after, there was a loud scream mixed with crying of a child who dropped his ice cream and didn't have any money to buy more. The crying stopped when an 11th grader gave the boy her ice cream and bought one for her from the extra money she brought. "Didi, I don't want this flavour I want the ice cream which you just bought", he said with the cutest puppy face. The eleventh grader rolling her eyes, gave him the ice cream and left, fearing he would demand more. Suddenly she came across two boys having a wrestling competition and the audience cheering them. Then realizing the captain(11th grader) is watching them, they stopped. The captain narrowed her eyes glaring at the two boys and left when her father came. And the busy afternoon turned into a usual honking of scooters and shopkeepers calling people to buy their grocery after long goodbyes of children to each other on their last working day.

CHAPTER ELEVEN

THE WOMEN OF INDIA

"So class, today we've got a new student from London with us, Amara Catherine. Please welcome her." The class applauded as Amara entered the rows and columns of chairs and tables looking for a seat and finally found one beside Jaya Gupta. "Hi" said Jaya. Amara replied "Hello".

It was not before two hours that the bell announcing the recess rung and Amara could see that everyone had already got their lunch boxes out on their tables minutes in advance. But everyone waited for the teacher to leave before they started pouring out of the class, down the stairs and finally in the open ground. "You can eat with us if you want to, Amara." said Jaya, to which, Amara replied with a yes. Soon they had found place on a bench and were having their lunch. Amara told her new friends, Jaya and Rishita how her father had decided to start a branch of his company in India, which was the reason why they had a transfer from London to Agra. "So, tell me something about India" Amara said after she had finished her side of the story. "India" Jaya started, "is not something that can be, you know, told about. You will see and learn the style and way of India. If you have any questions though, you can ask. I'll try my best to answer."

"Okay, so there's this thing that I haven't been really sure about. They say that women in India are not allowed to step out of their houses. Is that true? Because I see there are many female teachers in this school itself, I'm confused."

"Well, if you think about it, if women were not ALLOWED to go out, the teachers wouldn't be here, which means the are allowed, they just choose not to." said Jaya.

"But why?" questioned Amara.

"Look, in India, we have many goddesses. And according to the Geeta, which is our holy text of conduct, every woman is a goddess. They choose not to go out because if a woman goes out, Saraswati, the giver of knowledge goes out and ignorance might take shelter in the homes. If a woman goes out, Laxmi, the goddess of wealth goes out and poverty might reside in the house. If a woman goes out, Shakti, the goddess of strength exits the home and leaves the home in weakness. So some women decide to stay at home, while some women decide to go out in the society and be Usha, the goddess of dawn and a new beginning or Durga, the goddess who destroys the evil. And if a woman wants to do anything, you cannot stop her. Worship her and you will get the satisfaction of prosperity. You cannot force her to do something and if you do, she will be the reason for your demise. And I'm not saying that. This fact has its proof and roots growing back millenniums before today."

Amara was now deeply interested. "Whoa!" she exclaimed. Rishita grinned.

"But, I've also heard, that married women in India are not even allowed to shake hands." Amara shot another question at Jaya.

Jaya said "Does anyone shake hands with your queen in

England? "
" Only if she initiates. "
" That's exactly the case in India. In India, all women are queens. "

CHAPTER TWELVE

FEET OF WONDERMENT

"Radha, once there was a five year old girl, who was a very demure child. Every time somebody came to approach her, she either hid behind her mother's back or simply ran away. But there was one thing, which when she did, made her feel filled with aplomb. Nevertheless, she never did this in front of anyone, not even in front of the person whom she was closest to, her mother."

"Who was she and what was it that she never did in front of anyone?" asked Radha, the student of Maithili.

"That's me child. I was that girl and it's... Dancing. You know, whenever I used to dance I used to draw the curtains of my room and then dance. And till that time I didn't even know what dancing was. I just used to put on a music channel on the television and jump and hop with the songs. But do you know what happened one day? My mother soundlessly peeked through the curtains and saw me dancing! She didn't make even the lowest of a noise. When I was done dancing she came into the room, hugged me and said something that I couldn't forget until now."

"What ma'am?" asked Radha inquisitively.

"My baby girl has got feet of wonderment. These were her words. That time I did not understand what she meant. But today when I've grown up, I realize what she meant." said Maithili.

"What was it ma'am?" asked Radha.

"I'll that to you later. Let me continue what happened after that. My mother got me admitted in a nearby dance class for summer vacations but I developed more interest in dancing and continued going to that dance class even after my holidays. I still remember the first step I learnt from my teacher. Oh let me tell you, my teacher's name was Lucky. He was a brilliant teacher. But it was just then that I had got more interest in dance, that my teacher had to go to Australia for a dance workshop and after some time we came to know that he had settled there permanently. But my mother did not let that stop me from dancing. She found another dance class in our area. But this time it was a dance class that was completely dedicated to an Indian classical dance form. Kathak" explained Maithili. And when she said the word kathak, her voice was filled with pride. Pride for not knowing this dance form well, but for being associated to a dance form that was as deep as the sea.

"So now my dear Radha, when I come back from my tour after a month I want to see a different Radha standing here. A Radha who does not shake like a leaf out of fear when she's told to dance infront of other people. I want to see a Radha who is as confident as a bird committing itself to the air. Alright Radha?"

"Yes ma'am." said Radha while she wiped her tears.

Maithili hugged the little girl, both of them smiled and she bid goodbye to her student.

Well, Maithili was now a girl of 19. She was in one of the renowned colleges of the country and at such a tender age she had been able to achieve so much in the field of dancing. If one would talk about the awards that she had received, it would take hours to cover about all of them. Right after she passed her 12th standard and got into a good college, she decided that she is going to take out some time for dance. This time not just to learn dance, but to teach dancing to the underprivileged children. This was because she was aware that talent could be found anywhere, it does not see whether an individual is rich or poor. Within four months of taking this initiative she was able to build up a proper institute for dance, not just for the underprivileged children but also for the children who belonged to fortunate families. And the name she gave to her institute was inspired from the words said by her mother when she was a kid, “Feet of Wonderment”.

There were two upcoming dance events, or rather competitions that she had to participate in. One was in Bangalore, which was a competition among dancers who were specialized in various dance forms including the international dance forms. The other event was in Bhubaneswar, which was a competition among the dancers who were trained in various Indian Classical Dance forms.

First, Maithili went to Bangalore. She checked-in the hotel, got dressed up and left for the venue where the competition was going to take place. When she reached there, she came to know that she was the only one who was going to do a solo performance. Rest all the participants were either going to perform a duet or with their crew. She got nervous for a moment but then she told herself that she was capable enough to compete even against a ‘group’ of talented dancers and that was the reason she was here. When all the participants were called backstage, she went there and encountered something which she was mentally prepared for. A bunch of people who belonged to a breakdancing (an international form of dance) group approached her and said "There's no way you're going to win this competition. Your dance form is so ancient and easy. You shouldn't have come here."

Of course these words had hurt Maithili a bit, but she knew that something like this was certain to happen so she joined her hands and gave them a smile. They were a bit thunderstruck about how could someone give such a sweet reaction to such harsh words, but they went away from her.

Maithili was then engrossed in revising her steps when all of a sudden a couple, who was in a flamboyant dress, approached her. They joined their hands, bowed their heads and almost touched Maithili's feet but she prevented them from doing so. The dance form this couple did was Fadlango. It was a lively exuberant dance that belonged to the passionate land of Spain. The couple's eyes were filled with felicity and pride as if they've attained what was the prime goal of their life. They said, "Hi Maithili. We've been following you on social media from a very long time. We know how hard Kathak is to perform. It requires so much strength and stamina, but you do it so effortlessly! The grace that you put in your dance is just phenomenal. Your expressions, your gestures, everything is just so mind-boggling! And by the way you look absolutely gorgeous today. Like a Goddess!" Maithili was elated by their words and expressed her gratitude towards them. She also complimented the couple and their dance form. The couple then said "Toda la mejor!" Maithili didn't really understand what they meant but she passed a smile and thanked them. "Did you understand though what we said?" asked the couple. "Umm...no" said Maithili with an awkward smile. "Hahaha...that's 'all the best' " said the couple. “Oh! Well in that case, बहुत बहुत धन्यवाद और आज की प्रतियोगिता के लिए ढेर सारी शुभकामनाए!” replied Maithili. The couple was confused at this and Maithili could see it, so she translated it into English. They then understood that Maithili thanked them and wished them luck for the competition. The three of them laughed and laughed.

It was now time for the competition. Six group of dancers had already performed and it was now Maithili’s turn. The Spanish couple was greatly influenced by the Indian culture, so they were aware that before starting any good work, Indians eat curd and sugar. So they arranged it somehow and brought it for Maithili. “Dahi cheeni! exclaimed Maithili. “Thank you so much for this. I was just missing my mother right now. If she would have been here she would have definitely brought it for me right now. Everytime I have a performance, she bring this for me . I always refuse to eat it though, but everytime she convinces me and makes me eat it. She told me once that eating curd and sugar was not just an old- age practice but a healthy one too as curd acts as a natural coolant for our body, which helps fight the heat. At the same time, sugar is an essential source of glucose. When we have them together, it has a magical effect on our body! Oh I think I spoke a lot. But thank you so much. Really, thanks a million!” said Maithili. “Oh stop thanking us now. You’ve already done that a lot. It’s almost your turn. Go and perform well!” Maithili extended thanks to them and went towards the stage.

She first touched the stage, because without the stage, there would be no place to perform. This showed her immense respect towards the stage and devotion towards the art form. She then did the “Namaskaram” which she had first learned to do in classical dance, and ever since then she had been doing the same "namaskaram" before she danced. The soundtrack played, and she danced with all her heart. Everyone applauded for her once her performance was over. Even she felt gratified after her performance.

It was now time for the results. All the participants sat with their fingers crossed. Suddenly came the voice of the anchor, "At the third place we have...the Break Dancing Crew! At the second place is the Magical Couple from Spain. And at the first place....any guesses....Maithili Johri!!!!"

Maithili couldn't control her jubilation. She was called on the stage with the other winners and was honoured with the award. She was told to speak a few words on stage but before she could say anything, one of the members from the breakdancing crew came to the mic and apologized to Maithili for their direspectful conduct behind the stage and said that they have understood how powerful Indian dancing is, and especially Kathak. Maithili was delighted that she was able to change their perspective through her dance. She thanked her parents and teachers for their rock solid support and the organisation for giving her the opportunity to perform.

The event at Bangalore was successful,and now the event that was going to be held in Bhubaneswar was fast approaching. But since there was a week's time for that event so she came came to Varanasi to her parents. She told them about her victory at the event in Bangalore. Her parents were very happy to hear that. The atmosphere of the house was filled with euphoria. But something happened which made Maithili low-spirited. Her mother told her that she wouldn't be able to join her in the

Bhubaneswar event due to some unavoidable reason.

It was now a week that Maithili was at her place and now it was time for her to leave for Bhubaneswar. After a tiring flight she reached Bhubaneswar and then headed towards the venue where all the performers of the event were called for a meet up one day before their performance. When Maithili reached that place she was stunned. The venue was set by the side of a river, and there were hundreds of the dancers from various Indian classical dance forms present there. She felt as if she had joined her family now. A family whom she had never met but was always connected to by the strong bond of dance. She walked through them and went to that side of the river bank which was empty and dimly-lit. She could hear the sound of the waves of the river and the murmuring of all the people present there. The atmosphere felt magical to her and she started dancing on the beats of her surroundings. She danced with all her heart as if no one was watching her. All of a sudden the lights at the poles were turned on and she realized that people, who were no less than fifty in number were watching her with wide smiles on their face. Maithili was agitated. She had never felt so embarassed before. But the people were so warm and enthusiastic that they cheered for her and made Maithili feel like family. Maithili got comfortable at this and resumed dancing. But suddenly came the voice of a lady from the crowd, "STOP!!!"

Everyone was shaken with fear by the loud voice. This lady walked through all the people and it turned out that she was Maithili's mother. She said the same words that she had said 14 years back to Maithili, "My baby girl has got feet of wonderment!"

Maithili burst out in tears of happiness. She was in seventh heaven to see her mother as she didn't expect her mother

would come. All the people now cheered Maithili's mother too! It felt as if now the family reunion was complete.
Next day, Maithili's performance went wonderful. She made numerous new friends, got to know so much more about other forms of Indian Classical Dancing and felt immensely grateful for being a part of a country which had such diverse forms of art yet everyone was ONE! The concept of 'the beauty of the world lies in the diversity of its people' was now clear in Maithili's mind. She was of course very sad to leave Bhubaneswar and her extended dance family, but all of them promised to remain in touch with each other and for this purpose they formed a WhatsApp Group.

Maithili was leaving Bhubaneswar with bags full of memories and tons of love. She never felt so beatific and cheery after the completion of any dance event that she had been in till now. This was literally the best event of her life but there was one thing that troubled her- "Was she going to see a new Radha when she returns?"

CHAPTER THIRTEEN

BORN FROM THE DEAD

"102" The phone kept ringing "God damn it, Pick it up," said Aliya's mother with a painful voice.

It was Monday evening, and Aliya was doing her homework having no idea what was going on outside her room. It was 5 o'clock p.m. and it was time for her prayers. She thought "Where is mom, every time she comes to call me. Hand me over my burkha and we go for the prayers. Umm.. Forget it Aliya, maybe you are independent enough now."

She stood up slapped her books and went to her cupboard to take her burkha. She was about to leave her room when she heard the doorbell ring. Instead of going downstairs, she went to the window of her room to check who it was. But what she saw was not what she had expected. She quickly ran downstairs to see that her grandfather was unconscious and was taken to the hospital via ambulance. Tears rolled down her eyes, she wanted to go to the hospital but her mother denied it. As soon as the ambulance left she quickly grabbed her cycle and followed the ambulance. As the ambulance was fast she lost track of it. She reached there one hour later. And she was left aghast to see her grandfather covered with a white sheet. She started sobbing and ran to her mother to give her a tight hug. She wanted to see his grandfather for the last time but according to the Islamic culture, it was prohibited to see the body.

The whole family went to the nearby mosque.

The preparations were done and Aliya's father and her relatives were all set to start the funeral prayer service called 'Salat ul Janazah' in which petitions were offered to God asking for forgiveness for the sins of the deceased.

The time for the burial service arrived. The prayers and recitations of words and phrases from the Quran were expressed.

After the service, they all went to the family house to continue a time of prayer. Everyone was there except Aliya. She was in her room sobbing and seeing her grandfather's photos. When Everything started to fade and the next thing she so was she was lying on her bed and it was 7 o'clock a.m. and her mother was shouting at her as she was getting late for school. It took her 15 minutes to figure out all that she is so was just a dream. She was relieved and gave a long sigh and she couldn't stop herself to go and hug her grandfather.

CHAPTER FOURTEEN

THOSE DAYS

"Come my dear Soham, lie down on my lap. You must be tired, let me refreshen you with the tale of the day." Grandma was sitting on the top left corner of her bed with Soham on her lap as it was the time when she used to take some rest or tell stories to her dearest grandchild Soham. Her other two grandchildren, Sakshi and Sumit were studying in Boarding School so she always spent time with the eight-year-old Soham.

"Yes, yes dadi ,I am always excited for your ghost stories, and that Rabbit And The Turtle one, that's my favourite."

"Well, for today I am not going to tell any imaginary story. I am gonna tell you a real story. Story of my life."

"Oh, that's a song from One Direction, my favourite.", Soham started vibing. Grandma laughs,"Oh, my dear child, that was a good one.Okay, so are you interested in knowing, how school life was like back then? Did you know,we used nib pens for writing. These pens, which students use nowadays, are very different from them.There used to be an ink bottle in which we dipped our pens and then work. Till 5th or 6th standard, maybe till that standard, I don't remember much, we used pens called *kalam*. They were made up of a thin stick. We used to dip that in chalk powder." Then asuming, he would find it difficult to understand, she added,"Uhh, it was like P.O.P. I suppose you know that, right?" "Yes dadi. Of course I know." "Smart child. Now, during the examination time, when we used to finish our exams early, the teacher used to let us go out of class, while the other students completed theirs. And then we used to play hopscotch, gilli danda, skipping ropes, and what not , until our parents came to take us."

"Wow dadi, you could come out of the exam hall after you complete it!", he was amazed as he had to sleep or do anything to spend his time, whenever he completed his exam early, till everyone completed their's.

Grandma smiled,"Yes beta, and you know I lived in a huge haveli. I lived in a joint family. We used to have so much fun together. We were 4 real sisters and I had 2 real brothers also and rest were my cousins. You see this scar? I had this long time back. We were playing *'pakdam padai'* and I tripped and the scar became permanent. But it has so many memories attached to it." Soham noticed, grandma was smiling with her eyes closed. He could tell, she was feeling those times. "We used to have lunch and dinner together. Our mother and us sisters used to make food together.. As it was a large family;making food together, was so much fun." "Our father adored us immensely.Sometimes when we used to go to any occasion or party , he used to make us wear identical dresses(usually frocks) and we even used to wear the same perfume. Ah! those days. Soham, there's so much more to tell, but I feel sleepy now, and you must be having lot's of homework. Let us continue tomorrow." , she said yawning.

Soham felt so freshened up, and wished if he could also live those days. "Dadi, you spent your childhood so beautifully. I would love to time travel in the past and live one day there."

CHAPTER FIFTEEN

MILLENNIUMS TO COME

"Dadi! Story!" Cried Soham as he saw his grandmother get up from her evening prayers. It was her another day with her grandson and 'Dadi' and Soham could always be seen together from the time when Soham returned to school till bedtime.

"Yes my child, sure. What do you want to listen today?"

"Umm, you told me about past yesterday, now today, tell me about future."

"Future? Who knows future my son? Only God knows. Okay, I will tell you nonetheless."

"Yay!" Cried Soham as his eyes shone bright with excitement and curiosity.

"Now, before I begin, I want you to listen to this great verse from the Geeta.

यदा यदा हि धर्मस्य ग्लानिर्भवति भारत।
अभ्युत्थानमधर्मस्य तदात्मानं सृजाम्यहम्॥
परित्राणाय साधूनां विनाशाय च दुष्कृताम्।
धर्मसंस्थापनार्थाय सम्भवामि युगे युगे॥

In this verse, Shri Krishna says, 'Whenever there is loss of righteousness on this earth, acts of destruction take place and adharma progresses, then I incarnate on this earth.
I incarnate again and again in every age to protect all the good people and to destroy sin from the earth and to destroy the wicked and sinners and to establish dharma and bless all the people of the earth.

This is the story of India after more than 426 millenniums from now. When people will be so short they will have to use long sticks to pluck eggplants from trees. You know, an eggplant tree is just 18 to 24 inches in length. Imagine how short people will be at that time. That will be the time when evil will be at its peak. There will be corruption, hatred, theft, quarrels, fights, murders and what not. At that time, Lord Kalki, the 10th Avatar of Lord Vishnu will take birth in the home of the most eminent brahmana in the Sambhal Village. He will mount on his white horse named Devdatt with a sword of fire in his hands and destroy evil, bring peace in this world and do good to all mankind. This is the Great Legend of Kalki, mentioned in the Puranas."

"Whoa! I'll be waiting for him."

"Oh my child. Now go to sleep."

What Authors Have To Say!

"Want to be cognizant of various Indian places, cultures, traditions and lifestyle but can't tear up the miles to do that? Then this book is just the right thing for you. India is a fusion of multifarious vibrant cultures and colours. One can clearly distinguish the North from the South and the East from the West simply based on ethnic differences. But despite the differences we are one!

With so many varied languages, festivals, religions and traditions, India becomes more exotic and incredible to the rest of the world!

We the authors of the book realised that the country we live in has plenty of stories to tell. Infact every single corner has a story to tell, and thus the four of us got together and gave our very first attempt in writing a book.

Our book might be less in perfection but is definitely going to be more in authenticity!" ~**Inika Mohile**

"WALT DISNEY ONCE QUOTED THAT IMAGINATION HAS NO AGE AND DREAMS ARE FOREVER! We've got no age limits in our life. One can do anything anytime, and this MIRIAN CLUB of ours, proves it. Our teen group made up of a strong base, full ups and downs and never ending motivation given by each of us to each of us has written The FIRST BOOK which shows the rich culture and traditions of India, how life is spent in India, and what India has suffered since it's existence. WE HOPE YOU LOVE IT AND SEND US LOVE AND SUPPORT BY BUYING THIS BOOK AND RECOMMENDING IT TO OTHERS AS WELL." ~**Mishti Agrawal**

"This first book written by all of us has been an incredible experience and working with such amazing people made it all the way more special. This book definitely cannot sum up the integrity of India, but it definitely can show you the part of India that you might not have seen or heard of. No matter how much we develop or how drastic the changes are made politically or physically, but the roots of this country will stay the same. Its culture and traditions will always stay the same. It is said that everything changes, but some things never change, like the sun, the stars and India." ~**Ananya Singh**

I am so honoured to be a part of the MIRIAN club and to be a part of this wonderful and fascinating book. It was an incredible journey writing our first book ever "The Life In The Ethnic India", and working with this amazing group of creative writers. I would love to write another book with them. ~**Srishti Agarwal**

9 798887 337067

Printed by Libri Plureos GmbH in Hamburg, Germany